The Guardian

A Time Guardians Mini Mission

Plus

The Gorgon's Wrath

Also by Gareth Baker

Brackenbelly
and the
Beast of Hogg-Bottom Farm

Brackenbelly
and the
Dragon Duct Forest

✺

Time Guardians:
The Minotaur's Eclipse

✺

Star Friend

✺

Moggy on a Mission

✺

The Night I Helped Santa

Coming soon

Brackenbelly
and the
Village of Enigmas

Time Guardians:
The Centaur's Curse

The Lost Guardian

A Time Guardians Mini Mission

Plus

The Gorgon's Wrath

Nina,

Live for adventure!

09/10/19

Gareth Baker

First published by Taralyn Books in June 2018
1st Edition
© Gareth Baker 2018

ISBN-13:
978-1983444067

ISBN-10:
1983444065

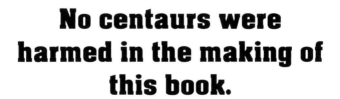

**No centaurs were
harmed in the making of
this book.**

If you are a new Guardian and not read *The Minotaur's Eclipse*, **please read the following information before beginning your adventures**…

Guardian and Equipment Profiles

Theo Harpe

Age: 12

The youngest ever member of the Guardians of The Net. As the 100th person in the bloodline of Theseus, he is the Kyrios ton Pithon, which means Lord of the Vases in Greek. Theo can communicate with the spirits of the old heroes and borrow their skills and abilities to help him complete his dangerous and vital missions.

Xever Harpe AKA Pappou

Age: 63

Theo's Cypriot grandfather, who lives in Cyprus. He is the 98th Guardian and protects the Hall of Heroes. His daughter (Theo's mother), never became a Guardian. Pappou has secretly been training Theo to become a Guardian since he was very young by telling him Greek myths, teaching him to scuba dive and many other useful skills. Theo and Pappou have always been close, but grew even closer after Theo's grandmother and father died.

The Hall of Heroes

The secret base of the Guardians, the Hall of Heroes is a cave hidden away in a secret location known only to the current Guardians. This hideaway is the home of two very important things. First is Oracle, the living spirit of The Oracle, an ancient fortune teller capable of seeing the future. She has access to all knowledge known to humanity and the gods. Second is the collection of ancient vases which hold the spirits of the ancient heroes.

The Sword of Chronos

Created by the gods, this weapon is not only super-light and super-sharp, it allows Guardians to create portals so they can travel through time and space. It is also used to send escaped beasts back to the Net. The Net is an energy field created by the gods to imprison the ancient beasts.

The Medallion of Morpheus

This gift gives a Guardian the ability to look like anyone he or she wishes. There are rumours that it is capable of much more, but that knowledge has been lost in the mists of time.

The Mirror of Aphrodite

Used by Guardians to communicate with each other or Oracle. The signal can travel through time as well as space.

The Lost
Guardian

The Mediterranean Sea, one week after

The
Minotaur's
Eclipse

"Right, Theo," said his grandfather, "you've had a week off, time to get back to work."

"I hadn't noticed it had even stopped, Pappou," Theo said, using the traditional Cypriot word for grandfather.

The week before, Theo had dramatically discovered that his family were part of a three-thousand-year-old secret society that was sworn to protect humanity from the beasts of ancient Greece. He had always thought the monsters were just stories – until he came face-to-face with the Minotaur.

Theo looked past Pappou and over the side of their battered, old boat. They were surrounded by the Mediterranean Sea. The island of Cyprus was far behind them.

That morning they had got up while it was still dark outside, got dressed in their wetsuits and then loaded the boat with the oxygen tanks and other equipment they would need for the dive. Now the sun was creeping up into the sky and Theo was further out to sea than Pappou had ever taken him before.

"Where are we? Is this another way into the Hall of Heroes?" Theo asked as he wiggled across the bench seat and positioned himself in front of his scuba tank.

"No. This is something different. We need a new vase to contain our ancestor, Theseus. His spirit is still floating about somewhere." Pappou looked at the sky above him. "Oracle pointed out yesterday that we needed to provide him with a new home after the other one exploded."

Theo remembered it clearly. Pappou had been injured but a flying piece of pottery, but the cut on his cheek was almost healed. Luckily it wasn't as bad as it looked, and neither was the pain in Theo's ribs after his encounter with the minotaur.

"I'm sure she did," Theo said, smiling at the thought of the bossy voice that seemed to fill the Hall of Heroes whenever she spoke.

"On the seabed below us is the site where the vases were found and rescued a thousand years ago," said Pappou.

"The ones in the Hall?" Theo asked. Shelves carved into the walls of the cave housed the ancient vases.

Pappou nodded.

"What do you mean, found? How did they get down there in the first place?" Theo asked.

"It's a long story, which I'll tell you later, but the ship that was bringing them from Greece to safety was caught in a storm and sunk."

"Unlucky," Theo said, though he was thinking that perhaps there was more than just chance behind the accident. With gods and monsters, most things were planned. "How long were they down there?"

"Over a thousand years. The Guardians searched for them for centuries, but then they were discovered quite by accident."

"By accident? How?"

"Well, I'm hoping that you will have a similar experience to Tallia, the Guardian who found them. She was out here fishing when it happened."

"All the way out here? What experience?" Theo asked. "What happened?"

Pappou's first answer was a wicked grin. Then he said, "Throw yourself in, and hopefully you'll find out for yourself. Don't fret, it's nothing to worry about."

"Okay. Can you at least tell me what I'm looking for?"

"Very well. All the important vases were recovered from the wreck of the ship, but other vases, which were filled with wine and used to disguise the sacred treasure while it was being transported, were left down there. They were all made by the same potter and it's my hope that one will make a suitable replacement home for Theseus. You may need to dig into the sand to find them, they've been there some time. Ready to go?"

Theo made an OK gesture with his hand and pulled on his diving mask. "Aren't you coming down with me?"

"Not this time. This is something you need to experience for yourself."

Theo sat on the edge of the boat and looked at his grandfather. Why did he keep using that word – experience. Was he trying to make it sound creepy? Or was he just winding him up?

Theo signalled he was ready, put his tank and flippers on, the rebreather in his mouth and, tipping himself backwards over the edge, dropped into the water behind him with a splash.

The sea was colder than Theo had been expecting, but then they had never come out this far from shore before. Despite the temperature, he welcomed it as it flooded his wetsuit and washed away the sweat that was making the black all-in-one suit stick to his skin.

Kicking his feet, Theo began to make his way down through the salt water. After a few strokes, he settled into a steady rhythm. His arms and legs worked together as a perfectly-timed team, giving him maximum power from minimum effort.

He had been diving most of his life. He had always thought his grandfather had been teaching him just for fun, but it seemed that almost everything they did was some kind of preparation for his role as a Guardian of the Net.

Down through the beautifully clear water, Theo saw the rocky surface of the seabed. It should be easy to find what he was looking for if the bottom stayed like that.

Fish scattered in every direction as Theo's passage disturbed the water around him. Their brightly-coloured tails — reds, blues and yellows — flicked and quickly carried them away to safety.

Theo stopped diving and looked up through the water. The bottom of Pappou's boat was easily visible above him, but he had swum down much further than he had thought.

How deep *was* it here?

A movement in the corner of Theo's eye drew his attention back to the bottom of the sea. A large flat fish with a long whip-like tail had taken off from the sandy-covered rocks and was swimming away, its wide, flat sides powering it through the water like a bird's wings.

A ray.

Theo knew it wasn't dangerous. Another of the many things that Pappou had taught him.

Now to find what I'm looking for. Theo swam through the spreading cloud of sand the ray had kicked up.

Was he searching for fragments of pots? The remains of a ship's mast poking up through a sand bank? The bones of the hapless sailor who had brought the ship from mainland Greece?

Theo waited. And waited. Whatever had led Tallia, the Guardian who had found them, to the wreck a millennium ago was not helping now.

Theo was about to move on, when it happened.

A bright flash burned his eyes and, for a brief moment, all he saw was blackness punctuated by long, wiggling red lines.

Disoriented, Theo held his position, suspended in the water, while he got his breathing back under control. Then he waited for the red lightning-like streaks to clear from his vision. Suddenly he was filled with an uneasy feeling as he realised he was vulnerable. At least Pappou would be watching from above, ready to act if need be.

The feeling soon passed and Theo felt a calming influence around him. It was the water. It was giving off the same peaceful feelings he had experienced when he had woken up in the Hall of Heroes for the first time.

Was that what Pappou had meant by 'experience'?

As Theo wondered about this, his eyesight returned to normal and he knew instantly that he had found what he was looking for. Before him was the most amazing thing he had ever seen (and he had seen some *amazing* things in his life even before he became a Guardian). A bright light hovered in the water in front of him. It was surrounded by countless fish that swam through it, creating a living, moving rainbow of flashing, glimmering scales.

Theo watched, wide-eyed, for a moment and then moved through the water towards the spectacle. The mass of fish and light moved away from him, keeping the one metre gap between them.

Okay, I get the message, Theo thought, stopping where he was. *You want your space. What are you?*

Theo felt the water before him shift as the fish darted around, repositioning themselves. Certain colours gathered together and then, before his very eyes, they formed a very life-like human face, as large as his bedroom window. Theo was so amazed, a stream of bubbles escaped his mouth.

The fish continued to swim, giving the face a shimmering appearance to its red lips, brown eyes and sun-kissed cheeks. As far as Theo could tell, it was a boy, perhaps only a few years older than himself.

Who are you? Theo thought. In the past, he'd been able to communicate with other heroes telepathically. Maybe he could talk to this entity too.

I am Dinis. What brings you here, Kyrios ton Pithon?

Theo watched as the fish forming the boy's lips shifted and moved in the water, mouthing the words, even though they came directly into his head with a thick Greek accent.

You know who I am? Theo asked.

Of course. Your essence is strong. Very strong. You must be the one, *the Kyrios ton Pithon.*

I am, Theo thought back.

He was the one-hundredth Guardian, and because of this he had a stronger link to the heroes in the vases than any Guardian before him. It meant he could call upon their power, skill and knowledge. What worried Theo was that when the Kyrios ton Pithon arrived on Earth, it also meant a great danger was on the way.

But he had already faced that and beaten it.

Hadn't he?

I ask again: what brings you here? said Dinis. *Be quick, my energy runs low and I am using yours to help maintain this form. I don't want to do it for too long, it could harm you.*

I come looking for more vases, Theo answered.

Tallia took them all. The heroes are safe once more, as you well know, Kyrios ton Pithon.

They're safe, don't worry. But one of the vases has broken and I need another. My grandfather, number ninety-eight, thought there might be some spare ones down here.

He's right. Quick I will show—

Dinis' voice stopped abruptly. Before Theo could ask him what was happening, the collection of fish began to separate and swim off, destroying the illusion of the face. At first Theo thought they were showing him where to go, but then he noticed the fish swam off in random directions.

The light had also disappeared.

Dinis? Theo thought. *Dinis, are you all right?*

I'm sorry to worry you. I could no longer hold that form. It was draining too much energy, but I can still communicate. Listen carefully and I will guide you with a single fish to the remains of my ship.

The ray Theo had seen earlier glided up off the floor. Somehow he knew it was the one Dinis was referring to.

You're the Guardian who brought the vases here? Theo asked.

I failed in my duty to get them to land, but then I met Tallia and showed her where to find them, just as I show you now. Come.

Theo looked up at the bottom of Pappou's boat one last time and followed the ray. It took him twenty or thirty metres away and then came to rest on the seabed, which Theo noticed had changed from rock to sand. In front of the ray's nose, the rim of a terracotta pot poked out of the white sand.

Theo moved towards it and the ray swam away. He reached down, grasped the top of the pot and pulled. And pulled. It would not come free. Placing his flippers on the ground, Theo manoeuvred himself so the pot was between his feet and tried again.

It was no good. It was firmly wedged in the sand. It *had* been there for hundreds of years, Theo reasoned.

He got down on his knees (not an easy task in the water) and began to scoop the sand away from the ancient piece of pottery. When he was satisfied he had removed enough, Theo pulled again. This time it came free, kicking up a cloud of fine sand.

Theo's sudden sense of victory was quickly replaced with disappointment. The vase was useless. The bottom half was broken off and missing.

He had to keep looking. Using the damaged pot as a tool, Theo began to scrape away at the sand, sending it swirling up into the water all around him until it was almost impossible for him to see what he was doing.

For all he knew, he might have uncovered a pot, he just couldn't see it.

He dropped the pot fragment and watched it disappear into the sandy water beneath him. Bending down, Theo began to feel the seabed in search of a vase when he felt himself sway forward as the water behind him pushed against him.

Had the ray returned? He turned his head, a stream of bubbles bursting from his mouth.

There was nothing there. Nothing that he could see through the murky water, anyway. The water pushed against him again, harder this time, throwing him to the side. Whatever it was, it was bigger than a ray.

A powerful surge of water came from his right. Theo turned, seeing a dark, indistinct shape through the murky water. Maybe it was Pappo. Perhaps he had seen the light and decided to come down and help him.

Theo swam out of the cloud and into the clear water.

And immediately wished he hadn't.

14

Staring straight at him was a creature that Pappou had always told him to avoid. Only this one was much, much larger than the ones he had seen before.

Its body was wider than Theo's shoulders, and at least twice as long. A rippling fin ran down the entire length of its long, cylindrical body. The nose, which was extended and narrow, sloped up as it joined its body, making its mouth look like it was smiling. But it wasn't a friendly expression. Its mouth was full of razor-sharp teeth.

It was a moray eel — and no ordinary one.

Theo began to move backwards as he struggled to keep his breathing under control. There was nothing he could do about his heart, which beat fast and powerful against the straps of his oxygen tank.

He knew the moray had a special jaw that allowed it to bite and then drag its prey *inside* itself. Not a nice way to meet your end. The jaws of this particular beast looked big enough to swallow Theo in one enormous gulp.

15

Theo almost spat out his mouthpiece in horror as the giant eel surged forward. Its wide head cut through the water as its jaw opened up ready to bite and swallow.

Theo twisted his body and brought his forearms up in front of his face to try and protect his mask and rebreather. The eel crashed into him, glanced off his upraised arms, sending spinning uncontrollably in the water.

A wave of nausea swept through his stomach as he fought to right himself. He ignored the pain in his inner ears and tried to relax. First, he had to get the rebreather back in his mouth, then regain his bearings, and then get away. But, by the time he got his feet back on the sandy ground and replaced the mouthpiece, the elongated predator had disappeared.

Theo spun around trying to locate the eel, making himself feel sick again. There was no point in swimming away in any old direction. He could find himself heading straight towards it.

He stopped and felt his blood run cold. He had found it. The beast was turning, ready for a second attack. Theo started to move but he knew he couldn't outswim it.

Dinis? If you're there, I need your help! Theo called out telepathically, hoping that the spirit of the Guardian was still out there. *I have a plan, but I need your help one last time.*

But no reply came.

Theo was on his own. Pappou was too far away too. He was going to have to rely on his own skills.

And he had just thought of a daring idea.

He stopped swimming and, keeping his eyes fixed on the eel, he unbuckled his oxygen tank. His movements felt slow and clumsy, like his fingers were numb and swollen, but at least they weren't shaking. With the rebreather still in his mouth, he held the tank across his chest, the straps facing upwards.

Come on. Come and get me if you want me, Theo thought, as he swam backwards so he could still see the movements of the over-sized eel.

It didn't take long for beast to take the bait. It surged towards him.

Theo braced himself. He only had one chance to get it right.

The eel's jaw opened, ready to strike.

Theo felt the water power towards him, pushed forward by the giant head that loomed before him. He waited until the last moment and thrust the oxygen tank up and then down again, making the straps open up as they trailed back down.

The sleek, pointed head of the huge fish swam through the gap, the end of its snout stopping just in front of Theo's nose. Theo pulled on the straps, tightening them around the eel's head, sealing its jaw shut.

Try swallowing me now, Theo thought, and swam away while the creature was trapped and distracted.

Knowing what would happen next, Theo took one last breath and then opened his mouth as the rebreather was ripped clear as the moray swam away, carrying the tank with it. Shaking its head from side to side, the eel tried to loosen the tank, but its mouth was held closed like a dog in a muzzle.

It was time to get back to Pappou and the boat. There was no telling how long the trap would last. Theo glanced at the eel one more time. It flipped its body, twisting in ways that no normal fish could, in an effort to escape.

No, Theo realised, it was also turning and coming in for another attack. It could still ram him. Its long tail powered through the water. Even the size and weight of the tank didn't seem to slow it down.

Theo kicked his way up, but it was already too late. A mouthful of precious air burst from Theo's lips as the moray collided with him, knocking him backwards through the water.

Theo grabbed the oxygen tank and held on with all his strength as the huge beast pulled him back down towards the bottom of the sea.

Pain shot through Theo as his back collided with the rocky surface of the seabed as the eel pushed him downwards harder and harder, its tail thrashing from side-to-side.

It was no good. He was pinned down and soon the air in his lungs would run out. While the eel couldn't eat him right now, he could still drown him and eat him later.

Theo felt his lungs protest as more air escaped his mouth. Stars appeared before his eyes as everything began to go black.

Dinis! Theo managed to call out in his mind. He could not hold on any longer. It was the end.

A bright pink light flashed through his eyelids and Theo thought he felt a wave of heat pass over his body. The only thing he knew for certain was that he was no longer pinned by the force of the beast.

20

Opening his eyes, Theo saw the eel writhing around in the water centimetres away from him, the rebreather hanging from the oxygen tank. To his side, the bright shining form of Dinis floated in the water.

Now, while I have blinded the cetus, Dinis called telepathically.

Theo grabbed the rebreather and took a deep gulp of oxygen. He had one final idea. He yanked on the pipe, separating it from the tank. A torrent of bubbles burst out of the nozzle, the stream so powerful it blasted the blinded creature away, gaining speed with each metre it spun and tumbled through the water.

Theo turned and looked at Dinis. His light was fading rapidly.

Go, while you can. It will quickly recover its senses and return. You must survive. There is great danger coming. Even bigger challenges than you have faced so far. Go…

Dinis faded away until there was nothing left but a bright spark of light that descended to the seabed. Theo looked in amazement. The seabed was covered with vases. The moray must have uncovered them as its tail thrashed around.

Goodbye, my friend, Theo thought, grabbing the vase Dinis had disappeared into and a second one for Theseus. With a powerful kick of his flippers, he swam up to the boat, thanking the gods this was the last time he would be scuba diving this holiday.

The Gorgon's Wrath

Six Months Later

An abandoned Greek island 876BCE

Sweat trickled down Theo's back. The air was hot. Very hot. And so was the stone column he was leaning against. Ignoring his discomfort, Theo poked his head around the tall structure and quickly took in the area before him. He ducked back into safety, closed his eyes and imagined what he'd just seen. It had only been for a few brief moments, but he had observed all he needed to.

The beast that had escaped from the Net was fifty metres away, curled up on a rock outside a cave, basking in the last of the day's sun. Her bronze breastplate glinted in the dying sunlight and her green, scaly tail twitched lazily. The snakes that covered her head also appeared to be asleep.

Good. That would make it all a lot easier.

Between Theo's position and the gorgon was a vast collection of statues and columns. Some looked like they had been here a long time. Some looked like they had been freshly created. Theo planned to use them to help him sneak closer to the gorgon so he could use the

Sword of Chronos and send her back where she came from.

That was the good news.

The bad news was that the statues had once been living people and animals.

Theo drew the sword and unhooked the shield he had stored on his back as he had travelled back through time. The gorgon had one deadly power. If you looked into her eyes, you turned to stone. That was why he had the shield. It had been Oracle's suggestion. And a good one it was too.

When Perseus had fought a gorgon called Medusa, he had used his shield as a mirror so he could get close enough to kill her without having to look at her.

Theo would not be killing her like Perseus had, but that did not mean his task was any easier. In fact, it would probably make it harder.

After checking that nothing had changed since he last looked, Theo carefully made his way to the first statue between him and the gorgon — a centaur, drawing back his bow as he reared up and aimed an arrow from the top of a large boulder. Theo tucked himself tight against the rock beneath the petrified hero. His heart beat so quickly he was afraid the escaped gorgon would hear it.

Would he ever get used to the excitement of being a Guardian of the Net?

Or the terror?

He hoped not.

"You fought the minotaur last summer and won. And the cetus. You can do this too," Theo whispered to himself before darting from the centaur to a toppled pillar.

He was ten metres closer to his target.

Peeking over the top of the fallen column, Theo planned his next move. Not far away there was a horse, forever trapped in its final moments, its rider toppling off its back. It would be large enough to hide behind while he decided on his next move.

Taking a deep, calming breath, Theo stepped out from behind the pillar — his legs bent, his head low — and ran to the horse and the unfortunate hero. He crouched in its shadow and enjoyed the comfort of the shade. After another quick check to make sure the gorgon hadn't moved, he sprinted to another column.

Safely there, he waited for his breathing to slow down before checking he was in the clear.

Theo's eyes widened and his mouth went dry.

The gorgon had gone.

Theo tightened his grip on the Sword of Chronos and told himself to stay calm. She could not have gone far.

A dark shadow fell over him and he instantly knew she was closer than he had thought.

"Wonderful. Another statue to add to my collection," came a hissing voice from behind him. "A human boy, no less. I don't have one of those... yet."

Move! shouted a voice in Theo's head. It was one of the heroes helping him, but not one he had heard before.

He had a good idea who would help him.

Theo immediately followed the advice and threw himself into a forward roll, tucking his shoulder into the shield, using the burst of hero energy that flooded through him thanks to his connection to the ancient heroes.

"Thanks. I'm guessing that's you, Perseus," Theo said as he scrambled to his feet and ran. He glanced into the polished surface in the back of his shield.

Yes, it is I.

"Come back," the gorgon screamed, swiping her tail through the horse's stone legs, destroying it and sending pieces clattering everywhere. Her anger spent, she slithered after Theo, sending pieces of trapped rock flying out from under her long, heavy tail.

Now he was getting a good look at her, Theo was shocked at the gorgon's size and strength. He

33

remained where he was, staring into the shield, mesmerized by her size, unaware that she was gaining on him.

Look out! Perseus roared inside his head.

Jolted into action by Perseus's advice, Theo swung the shield round to protect himself just as the gorgon's tail came at him. The disk of wood and metal rang out as it stopped the blow. Theo hardly had time to register he was flying through the air before he crashed to the floor, a tangle of arms and legs.

Get up and run, before she hits you again!

Theo got to his feet, doing his best to ignore the pain, and ducked between two frozen warriors. Without stopping, he leapt over another fallen column.

He was getting away, but it was no good. He *had* to gain control of the situation. He was a Guardian of the Net. It was his job to capture these beasts, not flee from them.

Theo looked into the shield again. The gorgon was off to the left, slithering around the end of the column he had just jumped over.

That was it. That was her weakness. She couldn't jump over things! That was how he could gain control.

Theo surveyed the collection of statues and stonework ahead of him and chose his route. He ran, weaving in and out of the sea of figures, leaping over more fallen columns, making the path as difficult and complicated for his pursuer as he could.

The terrible sound of smashing rock and the gorgon's screams of frustration filled Theo's ears as he arrived at her cave and rushed inside. He stopped and looked around. It was completely empty. He needed to find somewhere to hide and he assumed there would at least *some* furniture.

His eyes fell on the perfect place – an opening in the rock right at the back of the cave, wide enough for him to hide in and shrouded in shadow.

Theo squeezed himself inside and then, to his surprise found it was a cramped passage. Tucking himself down it as far as he comfortably could, he reached down the front of his top and grabbed the Medallion of Morpheus. He had an idea. He wasn't completely sure it would work, but the artefact from the gods was going to be crucial to his plan. It was a crazy, but it was the only one he could think of.

If he was going to beat her, he was going to have to *become* her.

Theo suddenly realised that the draw back of hiding was that he could not see her coming, so he held his breath and listened for her approach. Theo slowly breathed out of his nose and heard her scaly tail dragging across the stone floor of the cave.

"Come out, little boy, and meet your fate," she hissed.

Theo panicked. Did she know where he was? No, she sounded too far away. She knew he was in the cave somewhere. It was just a trick to get him to give himself up and come out.

"Very well, boy, I will come and find you. You're trapped! You'll make a nice decoration for my cave. It is a little… Spartan," she laughed at her own terrible joke.

The sound of her slithering scales echoed around the cave as she started to move again. Closer and closer she came to the crack in the rock until Theo was sure she was just outside his hiding place.

"Come out, come out, wherever you are," she called.

Now it was time to use the medallion and put the last part of his plan into action. Theo pictured the gorgon in his mind and stepped out of the crack, making sure he was looking down at the ground.

As soon as he saw her body, he shut his eyes and looked up, guessing where her eyes were. He had used the medallion to make himself look like a gorgon, and with any luck…

Theo heard the real gorgon's scream fill the cave. Then it was suddenly cut off.

His plan was working. It was actually working! A dull grey colour spread across her tail and up over her body.

By looking at another gorgon she was turning to stone!

Smiling confidently, Theo deactivated the medallion, powered up the Sword of Chronos and opened a buzzing, snapping portal right in front of his prize.

Now all he had to do was get her through it.

Theo went to step past her when something hard and cold touched his shoulder.

Don't look! Perseus yelled inside Theo's mind, stopping him from doing just that.

"Fooooooool," the gorgon cried, her words coming out slow and drawn out as if Theo was watching a DVD on half speed. "Diiiiid yooooou *reeeeally* thiiiiiink myyyyy oooown poweeeeeer wooooould wooooork oooon meee? Iiiiit wiiiiill sloooow meeeee doooooown foooor aaaa feeew seeeconds aat bessst."

"Then I better make them count," Theo said.

He quickly bent down, breaking free of her grip before it could tighten and ducked behind her.

"Enjoy being back in the Net," he cried as he leapt up into the air and summoned all the power and skill of Perseus and the other heroes in the vases. He unleashed a kick between her shoulders, sending her toppling forwards, towards the portal.

"No! You cannot beat m—" she managed to say before her final words were cut off as the portal closed, sealing her inside.

"That was too close," Theo said, wiping his arm across his forehead. "But we did it."

Yes, but it didn't look as satisfying as chopping off her head, Perseus said.

"Winning doesn't always mean killing," Theo said, repeating his grandfather's favourite saying.

True, but sometimes a trophy is nice, Perseus replied.

Theo will return...

Acknowledgements

This story would not have been possible without the considerable help, support and advice from many people. Of those, I would like to send special thanks to Nichola, The Covert Writers, Claire Tomkins, Chris Askham and Maria.

About the Author

Gareth Baker was a primary school teacher for 20 years. His childhood left him fascinated with heroes and their path of discovery and greatness. This is thanks to such films as Star Wars and The Three Musketeers. For most of his youth, Gareth grew up in the countryside on farms all over England, because his father was a shepherd. Today, Gareth lives in a world of his own, along with his family, superhero comics, books, films and computer games. He likes to deliberately say words wrong, plays the violin, the ukulele and Singstar. He looks forward to sharing his next book with you soon.

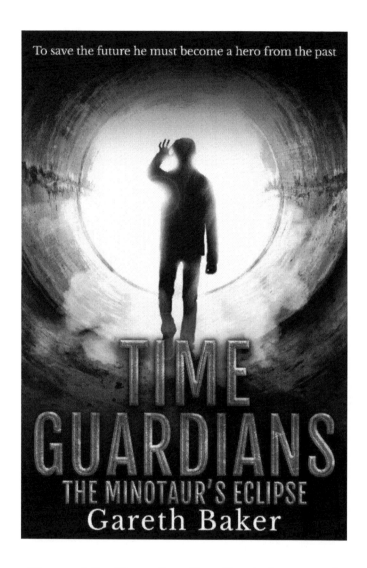

To save the future he must become a hero from the past

TIME GUARDIANS
THE MINOTAUR'S ECLIPSE
Gareth Baker

Travel in time for the first time and discover the secrets of the Guardians

New powers, new friends, new dangers

TIME GUARDIANS
THE CENTAUR'S CURSE
Gareth Baker

**Coming in 2018 -
The second full Time Guardians
adventure**

ROGUE RACER

GARETH BAKER

IN THE NEAR FUTURE, VR RACING IS
TAKING THE WORLD BY STORM,
AND SO IS THE MYSTERIOUS ROGUE
RACER

Travel to Kinmara and discover a world of excitement and adventure

Book 3 coming soon!

Find out more at

gareth-baker.com

Videos
Games
Activities
News

Sign up for the newsletter and get all the latest news

Follow Gareth on

Instagram - garethbakerpor
Facebook - /TaralynBooks
Twitter - @GarethBakerPoR

Thank You

43634175R00038

Printed in Poland
by Amazon Fulfillment
Poland Sp. z o.o., Wrocław